WHATEVER HAPPENED TO
MEGAN
MARIE?

Anne Schraff

PAGETURNERS

SUSPENSE
Boneyard
The Cold, Cold Shoulder
The Girl Who Had Everything
Hamlet's Trap
Roses Red as Blood

DETECTIVE
The Case of the Bad Seed
The Case of the Cursed Chalet
The Case of the Dead Duck
The Case of the Wanted Man
The Case of the Watery Grave

ADVENTURE
A Horse Called Courage
Planet Doom
The Terrible Orchid Sky
Up Rattler Mountain
Who Has Seen the Beast?

SCIENCE FICTION
Bugged!
Escape from Earth
Flashback
Murray's Nightmare
Under Siege

MYSTERY
The Hunter
Once Upon a Crime
**Whatever Happened to
Megan Marie?**
When Sleeping Dogs Awaken
Where's Dudley?

SPY
A Deadly Game
An Eye for an Eye
I Spy, e-Spy
Scavenger Hunt
Tuesday Raven

Development and Production: Laurel Associates, Inc.

SADDLEBACK
EDUCATIONAL PUBLISHING

Three Watson
Irvine, CA 92618-2767

Website: www.sdlback.com

ISBN-13: 978-1-56254-178-1
ISBN-10: 1-56254-178-1
eBook: 978-1-60291-222-9

Printed in the United States of America
15 14 13 12 11 10 09 1 2 3 4 5 6 7

CONTENTS

Chapter 1 5

Chapter 2 11

Chapter 3 17

Chapter 4 25

Chapter 5 34

Chapter 6 41

Chapter 7 48

Chapter 8 56

Chapter 9 64

Chapter 10 69

Chapter 1

Cathy North had been teaching U.S. history for four months now. She was the youngest teacher at Cascade High School and everybody's favorite. At 23, Cathy was just a few years older than her junior students. This morning, she was looking forward to her class with special enthusiasm.

A presidential election was under way, and the kids were giving oral reports. Cathy was expecting an especially good presentation from Megan Marie Kane. The bright 16-year-old had been lucky enough to actually interview one of the presidential hopefuls.

"You won't believe this, Ms. North," Megan Marie had excitedly told her teacher last week. "When Grandma took me to Washington last summer, we got a chance to talk to Senator Dean Mason in person! I've got some great stuff to talk about in my report!"

But when the first period bell rang, Megan Marie's desk was empty. She always sat front row center in every class.

"Does anyone know where Megan Marie is?" Cathy asked.

Everybody started looking around, expecting the eager, bright-eyed girl to come bounding in, her arms full of books. Megan Marie was sometimes late, but nobody could remember her ever being absent. She was every teacher's dream of the perfect student. Smart, friendly, respectful—always eager to participate. The presidential primary elections were just weeks away, and Megan's report was to be on one of the front runners, the charismatic Senator Mason.

After class, Cathy went over to the attendance office to see if Megan Marie had been reported sick by her parents. "She just *never* misses class," Cathy told the school secretary. "I'm concerned about her."

"No phone call came in from the Kane home," the secretary said as she checked a list. "Very few students are absent today. We'll be placing a call about her absence in just a minute."

Cathy usually used any break to go to the faculty room and grab a quick cup of coffee. But this time she lingered in the office while the secretary called.

"Well," the secretary was saying, "that's very odd because she never arrived at school, Mrs. Kane. . . . Yes, we're quite concerned, too. Please let us know if you learn anything. Of course we will." The secretary put down the phone, shaking her head. "Mrs. Kane said Megan Marie left for school at the usual time this morning. Mrs. Kane heard her drive away at exactly quarter after seven."

Cathy nodded. Megan Marie's schedule was like clockwork. Her snappy little red convertible always pulled into the student parking lot at precisely 7:30 A.M. She parked under the corner elm tree so the leafy branches would shade her car.

"Megan is such a creature of habit. She always parks in the same place, buys an apple or an orange at the fruit machine, and comes to my history class about four minutes before the bell," Cathy said in a concerned voice.

"Well, maybe she had a flat tire or some kind of car trouble on her way in," said Ms. Decker, the secretary.

Still a bit worried, Cathy went back to teach her next class. Then, during her next free period, she returned to the office to ask about Megan Marie again. Somehow she couldn't get the missing girl off her mind.

"No, I haven't heard a word," Ms. Decker said. "But you know how these teenagers are. Maybe on the spur of the moment she and her boyfriend decided to go to the beach. It's such a nice, warm day. If that's the case, you know, she'll get an unexcused absence."

Apparently, Cathy thought, Ms. Decker did not know Megan as well as she did. This girl would *never* skip school and go to the beach on a whim. Not Megan. She was far too responsible. Cathy was sure of that.

There was a special bond between Cathy and Megan Marie. Cathy figured it was because Megan was so much like she had been at the same age. Both Cathy North and Megan had short, curly blonde hair, big blue eyes, and dazzling smiles. They were pretty and popular, yes. But neither of them would ever put their social lives ahead of school.

They could have been sisters.

Cathy was becoming really worried. If car trouble had kept her from school, she would have called. If her parents had heard from her, they would have called.

Cathy feared that something must have happened to Megan Marie—something serious.

Chapter 2

When Cathy got home from school, she called Megan's home from her apartment. Cathy felt close to all her students. She was a brand new teacher, after all; she was proud of her work and felt privileged to be doing it. She loved the kids and wanted to teach them well. But she felt *especially* close to Megan because she was such a delightful girl and such a fine student.

"The Kane residence," a polite female voice said in accented English.

Cathy was momentarily surprised. Did the Kane family have a maid? Ordinarily, Cathy didn't pry into the students' personal lives. But she had never imagined Megan Marie as wealthy. "I'd like to speak to Mr. or Mrs.

Kane, please," Cathy said.

Within a few minutes, Mrs. Kane was on the line. "Yes?"

"This is Ms. North, Megan Marie's history teacher. I was concerned about her missing school today. Is everything all right?"

"No, it's not all right," Ms. Kane said in a high, nervous voice. "Megan Marie is still missing. We don't know where she is. We're calling her friends now. We hope they can help us. I'm really frightened. If she isn't home soon, we're going to call the police."

"Oh, no," Cathy said in alarm. "I'm so sorry—" Before she could say more she heard some kind of disturbance at the other end of the line. A man's voice broke in and asked harshly, "Who is this?"

"This is Ms. North, Cathy's teacher. I'm so sor—"

"We're very busy now," the man cut in. "I can't tie up the line. Goodbye." Then he hung up the phone. Cathy was startled by his rudeness. It was probably Megan's father, she thought. He must be under a lot of pressure, Cathy told herself, deciding that his lack of manners could be forgiven at a time like this.

Cathy put down the phone and sat on the couch. She was thoroughly puzzled. Megan had one of the highest grade point averages in the school. She was on the soccer team. She had a perfect attendance record. It didn't make sense that she had suddenly vanished on her own.

Cathy turned on the evening news. Senator Dean Mason was talking to a crowd in New England, whipping up support for the primary election. The man was Megan Marie's favorite candidate. She loved him in the way that other girls her age idolized a pop musician. Mason was a handsome man, perfect for a television campaign. He looked like a celebrity with his curly brown hair, twinkling eyes, and a grin that lit up the room. No wonder Megan was so thrilled to have met him in person last summer.

Megan Marie had been so eager to give her report today about the wonderful qualities of Senator Mason. Why wasn't she there to give it?

That evening, Cathy went out with her boyfriend, Jeff Martinez. He was a civil engineer, two years older than Cathy.

"The strangest thing happened at school today," Cathy told him. "One of my best students just *vanished*! Her family has no idea where she is."

Jeff laughed. "If I had a buck for every time I ditched school I'd be a rich man by now. And I was a good student. Sometimes the grind just gets to be too much and you need some breathing room," he said.

"But she's not that way, Jeff. She's a regular Miss Goody Two-Shoes. She's the kind of student I was—coming to class even when she's sick and really belongs home in bed," Cathy said.

"Great," Jeff laughed, mocking her. "It's sure *good* of you girls to spread your germs around to everyone else. Now *that's* responsible."

"Jeff, I'm really worried about her. It's not like her to just vanish," Cathy said. "I'm afraid that she was kidnapped or something. There are so many awful people around these days. . . ."

"Come on, Cath. You can't mother hen these little demons. Teenagers! Who can figure them out? Nobody could ever figure *me* out, I know that! She probably woke up this morning, heard on the radio that the surf was up, and took off to catch a wave," Jeff said.

"She doesn't surf," Cathy said.

"Whatever," Jeff said. "Listen, I hid out on my parents a couple of times. Hid out for two days in my friend's attic when I was 16—and all because of a fight I had with my father. This girl probably had a run-in with her parents.

Maybe she's taking time out to think."

"Jeff, you don't know Megan Marie as well as I do," Cathy said, a little annoyed by his flippant attitude.

"You don't know her, either, Cath. Don't flatter yourself. Deal with it. You like the kid, but you don't know beans about her life. She might be somebody entirely different when she's out of school. Maybe she's a heavy metal fan, and now she's turned into a roadie following some hottie band," Jeff said.

That night as she lay in bed in the darkness of her room, with no sound but the soft purring of her Siamese cat, Cathy thought about what Jeff had said. As much as his words annoyed her, Cathy had to admit there might be truth in them. Cathy saw Megan as a fine young lady and a bright student, but maybe there was *another* Megan Marie... one she knew nothing about.

Chapter 3

Cathy was anxious to get to school the next day. She hoped to see Megan's little red sports car parked in her favorite spot. But when school started and Megan didn't arrive, her hopes sank.

Cathy didn't know that much about Megan's personal life, but she had heard rumors that Megan was dating Don Zimmer, the star quarterback on the Cascade Cougars. Cathy had seen Megan and Don talking several times, and they seemed friendly. Don wasn't a great student, but he seemed like a nice enough boy.

Between classes, Cathy approached Don. "It looks like Megan Kane isn't here again today. Have you any idea where she might be?" Cathy asked him.

Don looked annoyed by her question. "How would I know, Ms. North?" he snapped.

"Oh, I just thought you two were friends, " Cathy said.

"No. I don't know anything about her," Don said. As Cathy walked away, she heard him say to a friend, "Megan Marie acts like she's such a hot babe that a guy should jump through hoops to get a nod from her. Well, not *me*! No girl is all that special. There are plenty of other tomatoes in the patch."

In the late afternoon, the school office was told that the Kanes had filed a missing persons report. When the teachers gathered in the faculty room after school, Megan Marie's disappearance was the main topic of gossip.

"Of course the police will treat it as a runaway," Oliver Ramirez, the young English teacher, said. "Whenever a 16-year-old kid disappears, the cops automatically always think *runaway*. And that's usually what it is, too."

"I can't imagine how they'd think that in this case," Cathy said. "Do you have Megan in your class, Oliver?"

"Yeah," Ramirez said. He'd already been teaching for eight years, and he'd lost most of his early enthusiasm for the job. There was too much paperwork, too much red tape, and too many kids who were bored stiff with school and didn't want to be there.

"Well, you *know* what a good student she is," Cathy reminded Oliver.

Oliver laughed. "You're still green, Cathy. You don't know what con artists these kids can be. Believe me, they aren't as innocent as they seem. Most of them are about 16 going on 30."

"I don't care what you say," Cathy insisted. "I'm afraid Megan Marie could be the victim of a crime. I'm really worried about her."

Cathy headed home, disappointed by the cynicism of her fellow teachers. She knew she probably shouldn't meddle in the private life of the Kane family. But around 7:00 P.M. she was so eager for news that she called their house.

"This is Ms. North again," Cathy told the maid. "Megan's history teacher. I'm concerned about what happened to her. Is there any news?" Cathy said.

"Just a minute," the maid said.

A man's voice came on at the other end. "Ms. North?"

"Yes. I'm so worried about Megan Marie. Have you had any news from her?" Cathy said.

"What exactly is your interest in our daughter?" Mr. Kane asked in a cold, unfriendly voice.

"Why, my *interest* is that she's a student of mine. I care deeply about my students," Cathy said.

"What did you say your name was?" Mr. Kane asked.

"Cathy North," she said in an uneasy voice. For some reason, the man seemed to be suspicious—even angry at her.

"Well, Ms. North, I find your interest in our daughter very strange. I must tell you that Megan Marie has picked up some very unusual ideas lately. She's been rebellious and mouthing all kinds of weird notions. We believe that teachers at Cascade High School must be indoctrinating the students with some dangerous agendas. I'll be coming down to the school to talk to the principal about it," Mr. Kane said.

Cathy was shocked. "I have no idea what you're talking about, sir. Why, Megan Marie is a bright, inquisitive girl who's a delight to teach."

"Yes, I can imagine. She'd be fertile ground for some of the wild agendas some of you teachers have these days," Mr. Kane said. "A bright but naive girl would be a prime target."

For a moment Cathy was too stunned to speak. Then she asked, "Have you heard from Megan?"

"I don't think that's any of your business, Ms. North. We'll be down there soon to find out just what the teachers at Cascade High School have been up to. We don't send our children to school to be recruited into some teacher's crackpot political agenda. And I would appreciate it if you did not call here again. Good evening," Mr. Kane said before hanging up.

Cathy was shocked. In the four months she had known Megan Marie, she had never heard the girl say anything strange. Megan was excited about talking to Senator Mason last summer—but he was certainly a respectable, middle-of-the-road politician.

For a long while Cathy sat wondering who Megan Marie really was. She had always appeared to be smart, well-adjusted, and happy—a pretty teenager eager to please, just as Cathy had been at that age. But the picture her father had painted was of a rebellious child full of wild, irresponsible ideas!

That football player Don Zimmer said she was a snob who saw herself as nature's gift to mankind. Who was she really? And *where* was she?

That night Jeff came over with a giant bag of popcorn to watch a movie on the VCR. Cathy now wondered if he hadn't been right on the money when he said she knew nothing about Megan Marie.

Then, just before the movie came on, the phone rang in Cathy's apartment.

"Hello?" a weird little voice said. It was a girl, but Cathy couldn't tell if it was Megan disguising her voice or someone else. "Is this Ms. North?"

"Yes. Who is this? Megan Marie—is that you? We're all so worried. Please tell me where you are," Cathy said.

"Tell Megan Marie's father that she's never coming back," the thin, reedlike voice squeaked.

"Is this you, Megan? Please talk to me," Cathy said. "Whatever is wrong, I'll help you." She still wasn't sure if the strange voice was Megan's or another girl's. Perhaps it was a friend who was hiding out with her. "Are you all right, Megan? Please—is Megan all right? At least tell me that much."

"No, Megan Marie is not all right. She will never be all right," the girl said. Then the phone went dead.

"Oh, Jeff!" Cathy cried, the color draining from her face. "Some girl with a weird voice just called me. She said to tell Megan's father that she was never coming home again and that she'd *never* be all right. . . ."

Frowning, Jeff pushed his popcorn aside. "Listen, Cath. I smell a rat. The kid must be holed up with her buddies, and now they're playing mind games. Don't get mixed up in this fiasco. It's not your ball game. Call the police. This little twerp could get you into a mess of trouble. Believe it!"

Chapter 4

"Do you think I should call Mr. Kane like the girl said?" Cathy asked.

"No way, Cath. Just call the police. Let them handle it. Then try to forget about it," Jeff said.

Cathy thought that Jeff probably knew best. So she called the police department, and a Detective Twyla Moore came on the line. The officer said she was in charge of missing teenagers, presumed runaways. Cathy told her exactly what had happened.

"Did you recognize the voice of the caller?" Detective Moore asked. "Do you think it might have been the Kane girl herself?"

"I couldn't tell. It *might* have been Megan disguising her voice. Or maybe it was somebody else. I'm just not sure," Cathy said.

"Well, thank you for calling in the information," the detective said. "We'll look into it."

Jeff was laughing and shaking his head as Cathy hung up. "Don't you see what's coming down here, Cath? This little jerk has a scam going. She runs away, hangs out with a girlfriend, and they send cryptic messages to her father, trying to yank his chain.

"Maybe she wanted to spend next summer in Mexico with her boyfriend— and her parents vetoed it. Now she's getting even. She wants revenge on her mean, evil parents. See, *all* parents are mean and evil these days. They do cruel things like not letting their kids stay out all night and get drunk. Then the kids get mad and run away, so they decide to make their parents sweat . . . that's all this is, Cath."

"I just can't see Megan Marie doing

such a thing, though," Cathy insisted.

"That's because you're such a sweet little cupcake yourself. You never *were* a typical teenager!" Jeff laughed. "That's why you refuse to accept what little monsters kids can be!"

"No, Jeff, you're wrong. I think Megan was kidnapped. Her parents are rich and she's been kidnapped. The kidnappers could be softening up the parents before they make their money demands. I bet right now that poor girl is tied to a chair in some dark room. She's probably blindfolded and frightened out of her wits," Cathy cried.

Jeff stuffed his mouth with popcorn. "Yeah, *right*! And the moon is made of pizza pie. Cath, right now Megan is sprawled in front of a television set somewhere, watching some airhead teen sitcom," he mumbled as he shoved in another handful of popcorn.

Cathy was annoyed. "How did you get so cynical, Jeff?" she asked.

"Hey, I was 16 once, Cath. If I had been my dad, I'd have *killed* me! I can't believe my parents still talk to me after some of the stuff I did. They must be saints," Jeff said.

Cathy didn't expect Megan Marie to be in school the next day, and she wasn't. Every time Cathy looked at the desk where Megan Marie always sat, she felt a pang of sadness. Yet all day Cathy kept telling herself that she couldn't have been that wrong about the girl. She just *couldn't* have been!

Then, in the afternoon, the principal asked Cathy, Oliver, and Daisy Stevens, the PE teacher, to meet in her office for a conference with Megan's parents.

Cathy was nervous as she walked down the hall. She had had no contact with Megan's parents before this. It wasn't unusual for parents of high schoolers to avoid things like parents' night. Now Cathy wondered what on earth had given Megan's parents the idea that she or any teacher at Cascade High was brainwashing their daughter.

Cathy had never had a political agenda herself. She was from a middle-class family with middle-class values. She sang in the young people's choir at her church and volunteered once a week at a downtown soup kitchen. When election time came around, she voted for people, not parties. Cathy wouldn't have recognized a weird political agenda if it hit her in the face.

Megan Marie's parents were already seated in the principal's office when the three teachers arrived. Ms. Buckthorn, the principal, sat at the head of the table. She introduced everybody, and then she turned to the Kanes. "What concerns do you wish to express?" she invited.

Mrs. Kane was a slim, small woman. She had large brown eyes and a darker complexion than her husband. She reminded Cathy of a little animal cowering in a dark corner, afraid of her own shadow. Maybe, Cathy thought, that was a totally false impression, but that's the impression the woman gave.

Mr. Kane was tall and muscular. He looked like he could have played football in his youth. Obviously, his blond good looks had passed down to Megan Marie. She looked just like her father.

The Kanes were young parents, perhaps only in their late thirties.

"Well," Mr. Kane said, "before Megan Marie came to Cascade High School, she was a wonderful girl. She was happy, content—everything parents could ask for. She did what we asked her to do without question. Then, a few months ago, she began to change. She started questioning our right to tell her anything.

"She had this stock phrase: '*I don't have to listen to you. I have a right to my own ideas.*'" Mr. Kane's face reddened in anger. "We believe that a teacher here at school was encouraging this rebellious attitude. This teacher must have been encouraging students to disregard their parents. You know what I mean—children's rights and all that rubbish! We believe that Megan Marie was corrupted right here—and as a result, she's now run away from home and is hiding out somewhere!"

Ms. Buckthorn turned to the teachers. "Well, what can we say about Mr. Kane's concerns?"

Oliver had a sneer on his face. "Listen, I'm so busy trying to teach English to 38 kids who'd rather be at the beach, that I wouldn't even have *time* to indoctrinate them—even if I wanted to, which I don't. I've got all I can do trying to teach them to write a coherent sentence." He looked directly at Mr. Kane. "Your daughter struck me as a typical teenaged girl. I never heard her talking about children's rights or any other ideas like that."

Daisy Stevens seemed very frightened

by this meeting. She had never been suspected of any wrongdoing before. As a single mother trying to support two children, she was terrified of anything that threatened her job. It was obvious that she was afraid these people would make trouble for her.

"Megan plays soccer very well, but we never get into politics in gym class. She admired those American girls who won the World Cup games. She had a t-shirt with one of the player's pictures on it. Once she said that she hoped to play soccer in the World Cup games someday. I promise you there was nothing about politics in my class—*nothing*!"

Mr. Kane turned his attention to Cathy. "Megan was always talking about you, Ms. North. She idolized you. Whenever I turned around, it was *Ms. North this, Ms. North that*. I got sick of hearing your name. I strongly suspect that *you* were the one who put these rebellious ideas in her head! I believe we have you to thank for losing our only daughter. I hold you responsible, Ms. North, and I am angry."

Mr. Kane's face tightened and his voice shook with righteous indignation. *"I hope you are happy, Ms. North. You have destroyed our family!"*

Chapter 5

Stunned, Cathy looked steadily back at the angry man. "I teach U.S. history, Mr. Kane. I have no agenda except teaching U.S. history and helping my students become good citizens. If Megan had rebellious ideas, I didn't notice them and they certainly didn't come from me," she said assertively.

"Megan Marie never questioned my authority until she met you, Ms. North," Mr. Kane said bitterly. "Suddenly I was not a good father. I was not a good husband to my wife. I was doing everything wrong, and I had to change." He turned to his wife, who had been totally silent until now. "Isn't that what happened, Mimi?"

"Yes," Mrs. Kane said nervously, her

eyes darting around the room as if she were looking for a way to escape. Her hands tightly folded in her lap.

"I believe Megan Marie learned these rebellious ideas in your class, Ms. North. I am outraged," Mr. Kane said.

Ms. Buckthorn spoke up then. "Mr. Kane, I am terribly sorry that such a tragic thing has happened to your family. But I don't believe you can blame any member of my staff. I visit all the classrooms, and I've never heard *any* sort of political agenda being fostered— radical or otherwise. I wouldn't put up with it. I'm sure that your daughter decided to do what she did based on her own feelings," she said.

"Well, I didn't expect any satisfaction here," Mr. Kane said disgustedly. "You people all stick together. I expected that. But if we've lost our daughter, I intend to expose the people responsible. I'm going to blow this thing wide open. I've heard about schools pushing their political agendas into innocent young minds, turning children against their parents. . . *I won't stand for it!* I can promise you that."

Then Mr. Kane stomped from the room, followed meekly by his wife. When the office door was closed, Ms. Buckthorn said, "Thank you all for coming. I'm sorry you had to go through that, but he insisted on a conference."

The three teachers were shaken as they returned to the faculty room.

"Can you *believe* that blowhard bully?" Oliver cried, pouring himself a cup of black coffee.

"And that poor wife of his," Cathy said. "She acted as if she was scared to death of something."

"That's the meanest man I ever saw," Daisy said, shuddering. "He's even worse than my ex-husband was."

"I can't imagine what he's talking about," Cathy said, pouring milk into her coffee. A few minutes later, she hurried out to her car for the drive home. She was exhausted—more tired than she ever remembered being. It had always been a joy for Cathy to come to school. She had *loved* teaching her classes. But the mysterious disappearance of Megan Marie now hung like a pall over the whole school.

As Cathy approached her car, she spotted Rita Dobbs, a quiet little junior, walking toward the bus stop. It dawned on Cathy that she had seen Megan Marie and Rita having lunch together many times. Rita was a shy loner. Cathy had always assumed that Megan reached out to her out of kindness. Megan was that way. She seemed to have a big heart for underdogs. Maybe that was one reason she liked Senator Mason. He often talked about reaching out to the poor, the uninsured, the sick.

"Oh, Rita," Cathy called out, "may I have a word with you?"

"Yes, ma'am," Rita said, turning. Her

hair was long and stringy and she wore cheap, mismatched clothing. In a school like Cascade, where most of the kids were from middle-class homes, Rita stood out. She was frequently the butt of jokes. The other girls got their clothes at trendy teen shops in the mall. Rita shopped at the thrift store downtown.

"Rita, I'm really worried about Megan Marie. Did she ever say anything to you that hinted she might run away?" Cathy asked.

"Is that what you think she did, ma'am—ran away?" Rita asked in her soft, forlorn voice.

"I don't know, Rita. What do you think?" Cathy asked.

"I guess that's what happened. She must have run away. She was sad sometimes. I guess she got sadder all of a sudden. I don't know," Rita said. Shrugging, she turned around and continued on to the bus stop.

Cathy drove by the Kane house

before she went home. She had never seen the house where Megan lived before. It was a beautiful multilevel building set back behind an expansive lawn and gardens. The lawn was a perfect green carpet, and many colorful roses bloomed along the flagstone walk. Cathy thought about it. This was the house Megan left every day in her little red roadster. It would seem that she had been a lucky girl. Her own sports car at 16, a beautiful home to live in. What would make her run away from that?

Maybe she *didn't* run away, Cathy thought as she drove away. Maybe everybody was wrong, including her parents. Maybe something awful had really happened to Megan Marie Kane.

On Saturday morning Cathy had just finished washing her hair when the local news came on the radio. The news woman first gave the headlines. "Has there been a major breakthrough in the story of missing teenager Megan Marie

Kane? More in a minute."

Cathy wrapped a towel around her head, her knees going weak. She sat down near the radio, clasping her hands nervously.

"A red sports car belonging to missing local teenager Megan Marie Kane has been located in 20 feet of water alongside the causeway. Details are sketchy at this time, but the police have promised a news conference for later in the afternoon. There is no confirmation yet that the girl—or her body—has been located. Megan vanished on her way to classes at Cascade High School on Monday morning. She was last seen at a convenience store near the causeway at about 7:00 A.M. Stay tuned for more information as it becomes available."

"*Oh no, oh no!*" Cathy groaned, burying her face in her hands.

Chapter 6

Between Megan's house and Cascade High there was a causeway bordered on one side by a lake. Cars had slipped into the lake before, usually on rainy or snowy nights. Two tourists had been lost there several years ago. Could Megan have simply lost control of her car, skidded into the lake, and drowned? That would explain everything—*except* the strange phone call Cathy had received from the squeaky-voiced girl.

Or had someone witnessed the accident but not been willing to come forward? Could that be it? Maybe it was a girl from school. She might have called Cathy just to let her know that Megan was never coming home.

Jeff came right over after Cathy called

him. He hadn't heard the news about the car, and he looked shaken. Up until now, he had been so sure the whole thing was a teenage prank.

"Jeff, they found Megan's car under 20 feet of water," Cathy cried. "The news just came in over the radio."

"Oh, man . . . she's dead, huh? I'm sorry, Cath. I know you liked the kid. That's a real bad break." Jeff rubbed Cathy's back soothingly as he held her in his arms.

"They haven't found her body yet," Cathy said. "I'm hoping that somehow she still made it . . . that she jumped or something."

"Hey, Cath, maybe you better not go down that road. Better face reality. After all, nobody has seen the kid since Monday. Where is she if she's not—*you know*," Jeff said.

"Jeff, it's *so* not fair! She's only 16 years old. She has her whole life ahead of her," Cathy groaned.

"Sometimes life isn't fair, honey. I had a sister who died when she was only 27. That wasn't fair either. But you have to learn to accept it. Then you go on and make the best of it," Jeff said.

By midmorning they still had not found a body. Cathy's hopes rose. They were dragging the lake near the accident scene in case she had fallen from the car and been carried away by the currents. That's what had happened to the tourists who were lost. Their bodies weren't recovered for a week, and then they were far downstream.

On Monday everybody at school was talking about Megan Marie Kane, even kids who didn't know her personally.

One girl said, "I bet she faked the accident, hoping everybody thinks she's dead—or maybe she wanted to run off with her boyfriend." Her friends joined in the speculation.

"She really liked that Senator Dean Mason," one of them giggled. "Maybe she's with him. He's that really cute guy who's running for president, you know. Megan was totally in love with him. Maybe she's gone to New England to help him with his campaign."

Everybody laughed at that and added more speculation.

Cathy tried to tune out all the talk and concentrate on her classes. At the end of the day she was exhausted. All she wanted to do was go home and soak in a hot bath. But when Cathy got home, before she even had time to drop her purse on the end table, the phone was ringing.

"Cathy North?" an oddly familiar woman's voice asked.

"Yes," Cathy said, "who is this?" She was sure she had heard the woman's voice before, but she couldn't place it.

"This is Wendy Birdsong—you've probably seen me on the 6:30 news," the woman said.

"Oh, yes," Cathy said, wondering

why in the world this newswoman was calling *her*. Birdsong was a beautiful blonde whose witty repartee with her co-hosts pushed up the ratings of her station. "I see you all the time."

"Well, we're doing a feature story on the girl who has disappeared—Megan Marie Kane—and we understand she was quite close to you," Birdsong said.

"She's one of my best history students. I think she's a lovely girl," Cathy said, "but I have no *personal* relationship with her. Are you sure you want to talk to me?"

"Well, would you be willing to say a few words about her on camera if we came over to your place in . . . say 25 minutes? We'd like to get you on the 6:30 evening news. From what we've heard, you were her favorite teacher," Birdsong said.

Were? Cathy shuddered. Wendy Birdsong was talking about Megan in the past tense! "I guess it would be all right

45

for you to come over," Cathy said.

"Thank you. We'll be there right away, just me and the camera guy. We won't take up much of your time at all, and we really appreciate your help," Birdsong said.

Cathy put down the phone, thinking about something she might say about Megan that could help find her if she was still alive. That was the only reason Cathy agreed to the interview.

The news anchor and her cameraman arrived 20 minutes later. In the flesh, Birdsong did not look as flawless as she did on television. The wind had wreaked havoc on her hairdo. It was a warm day and she looked a little flushed from running around. Her creamy complexion was marred by a tiny pimple on her chin. But after some last-minute touchups, she began the interview.

"Ms. North, you teach history to Megan and probably know her fairly well. Did you notice anything unusual about her the last time you saw her on Friday?" Birdsong asked, thrusting the microphone at Cathy.

"No, she was just her normal self," Cathy said. Blinking in the bright lights, she was more nervous than she thought she'd be.

"We've heard that your classes stress the idea that teenagers are independent people with rights of their own. You teach that they have every right to speak out against things they don't like in their homes. Do you worry now that you might have encouraged Megan to take this too far? Did the course you're teaching encourage her to run away from home?" Birdsong asked.

Cathy was stunned. She had never expected such a blunt question. Wendy Birdsong was taking it for granted that Cathy taught kids to rebel against their parents!

Chapter 7

"No," Cathy stammered, "I just teach history."

"But isn't it true that you urge your students—especially the girls—to be more assertive? Aren't you concerned that Megan may have taken that too much to heart?" Birdsong's voice became more aggressive.

"No, no!" Cathy cried, knowing she was looking weak and dishonest. "Nothing like that happens in my classes!" She couldn't believe the interview was turning out this way. She wanted to turn around and rush back into her apartment, but she knew that would make her look even worse.

"Megan's parents have told us that you spend a lot of time on women's rights and children's rights," Birdsong hammered. "Is it possible that Megan took these ideas too far?"

Cathy felt defensive, and she knew she sounded that way, too. "Once we had a class discussion about women in ancient times—how they were *owned* by their husbands. I simply pointed out that women and children now have legal rights. We had this discussion, but there was nothing more about it," Cathy said.

"Thank you so much, Ms. North," Birdsong said, ending the interview. She smiled, and then quickly turned and marched down the driveway on her chunky high heels.

Cathy stood there, feeling as if she had been hit by a truck. She could only stare at the white panel truck with the call letters of the television station emblazoned on the side.

Just as the television truck drove off, Jeff pulled up at the curb.

"Hey, what was *that* all about?" Jeff

asked. "You a celebrity now, Cath?"

"I was just ambushed, Jeff. I was set up by that horrible sneaky woman and ambushed!" Cathy groaned.

"What are you talking about?" Jeff asked as his smile faded.

"Wendy Birdsong asked if she could talk to me about Megan. Then she shows up and practically accuses me of brainwashing the girl. She implied that I was *responsible* for her disappearance! I was only willing to be on TV if it could help find Megan—but that woman was out to hang me!" Cathy cried.

Jeff stayed with Cathy until the 6:30 news came on. They had heard the promotional teaser on the 5:00 P.M. news. In her usual breathless voice, Birdsong had said, "Shocking allegations from the parents of missing teen Megan Kane whose automobile was found in the causeway lake today. At 6:30, we'll have exclusive interviews with the parents and an accused teacher."

Cathy almost dropped her coffee cup. "Oh, Jeff! Do you think they'll let that awful Mr. Kane tell all those lies about me on television? Surely they wouldn't be that irresponsible. . . ."

"Better hang onto your hat, Cath! They'll put *anything* on that they think will grab the viewers. The more sensational the better," Jeff said grimly.

When the 6:30 newscast came on, Wendy Birdsong was wearing a serious, concerned expression on her pretty face. Usually she had a broad smile and a bubbly laugh, but now her voice was stern. "The distraught parents of missing Megan Marie Kane have agreed to talk exclusively with us today. The popular Cascade High junior has been missing for a week now. This morning her car was found under 20 feet of water off the causeway. No body has yet been recovered. But now Megan's parents are charging that a radical political agenda at their daughter's school may have led to her recent disappearance."

The scene shifted to the elegant living room of the Kane house. Mr. and Mrs. Kane were shown sitting on their couch. A large framed photograph of Megan Marie was prominently displayed on an end table.

"Mr. Kane," Birdsong said, "what would you like to say to your daughter if she can hear you now?"

"Megan," Kane said, "we love you. Whatever you have done, we love you. Please come home."

"And you, Mrs. Kane," Birdsong said, "have you anything to add?"

The sad-looking little woman was crying. Cathy noticed that her nose was a little bumpy and uneven, but still she had a very pretty face.

"I just . . . hope she's all right," she said, her voice breaking.

"Mr. Kane," Birdsong said, "you called the newsroom with some shocking allegations against Megan Marie's school.

What are your concerns exactly?"

Cathy groaned aloud. "Oh, wow, Jeff—here it comes!"

Jeff tightened his arm around her shoulders. "Don't worry. The truth is gonna come out," he whispered.

"Yes," Kane said, "there's a history teacher at Cascade High who seems to have been pushing her political ideas. She's been undermining the authority of parents and encouraging rebellion among these kids. We think Megan ran off and ditched her car in an act of rebellion against us—fostered by this teacher and her wild agenda. Cathy North has been going too far!"

Birdsong looked into the camera then and said, "This morning, we talked to Ms. Cathy North, the history teacher that Mr. Kane referred to this afternoon. We offered her the opportunity to respond to these serious charges."

Suddenly Cathy was seeing herself on camera, looking bewildered and frightened, her hair mussed by the wind, her eyes wide. Birdsong led into the bit by saying, "Ms. North denied teaching anything improper to her students, although she admitted her strong views on women's and children's rights. . . ."

Cathy appeared again, mumbling about ancient times, how women were once owned by their husbands, but, of course, now have legal rights.

Birdsong returned, "So, as the worried parents of Megan Marie Kane wait for word of their daughter's fate, they wonder if the lessons she learned in her high school history class might have led to this tragedy."

"*Jeff!*" Cathy groaned as the next segment began. "She didn't use any of my denial of teaching teenage rebellion. She just used what made me look bad! Nothing could be farther from the truth.

"Oh, Jeff, how did this happen to me? Everything was going so well with my job at Cascade. I *love* to teach! I was getting good reviews from the principal and the kids liked my classes. Now, Ms. Buckthorn is going to think I'm a dangerous fanatic leading kids away from home like some crazy Pied Piper."

Jeff tried to comfort her. "You always told me Buckthorn was a down-to-earth lady. She'll see through this, Cathy. And as soon as the missing girl shows up, she'll tell the truth. Then everything will be explained once and for all," Jeff said.

"I've *got* to find her!" Cathy said with sudden resolve. "I've got to rack my brain for everything I can remember about her. There *must* must be some clues to where she might have gone!"

"I'm not so sure. If she was desperate enough to let the car slide into the drink, maybe she doesn't *want* to be found, Cathy. There must be something really *wrong* in that family to have driven a kid to this," Jeff said.

Chapter 8

Cathy pressed her fingers into her temples. "Let's see . . . Megan loved jazz music. She seemed to like Don Zimmer—but he denied that they had a close friendship. Megan thought that guy running for president, Senator Mason, was just about the most wonderful person on earth.

"She also had a ton of books about President John Kennedy. He was her sort of hero, even though he died before her *mother* was born. One time Megan talked about how kind and compassionate Senator Mason seemed to be. She thought he'd bring back the days of Camelot. . . they used to call the Kennedy years *Camelot*, you know."

"Is her favorite candidate married?"

Jeff asked her with a small, wry grin.

"Oh, Jeff! Of course he is! He's 44 years old, and he has a wife and three kids. I just meant that Megan hero worshipped him," Cathy said.

"He's popular, all right. I keep seeing him on TV, campaigning all around the country," Jeff said.

Cathy sighed. "Megan would never cause all that trouble by running off to New England to campaign for her hero! She must have been running away from something *personal*. I need to find out more about that family of hers."

"How are you gonna do that, Cath? You're not a detective," Jeff said.

"Maybe I could talk to some of their neighbors," Cathy said.

Jeff frowned. "Oh, man, don't you think the Kanes already hate you enough? Now you're going door-to-door snooping on them!" he said.

"Jeff, you don't understand! Mr. Kane is ruining my reputation. He's putting my teaching career in jeopardy. I studied for five years to become a teacher, and I love it. I'm not letting him undermine me with his lies! Besides, I *care* about Megan Marie. She's a 16-year-old kid out there someplace—most likely trying to survive on her own. Maybe something I can dig up will help us find her," Cathy said.

Jeff threw up his hands. "Okay, Sherlock, where do we start?"

Cathy smiled and put her arms around Jeff, giving him a big hug.

An elderly man came to the door at the house directly east of the Kanes. But he was gruff and refused to talk. He slammed the door on Cathy and Jeff.

Just west of the Kanes lived the Websters. They were a middle-aged couple with grown children. When Cathy and Jeff introduced themselves as private investigators looking into Megan Marie's disappearance, the Websters invited them in.

"I don't know what we could tell you that would do any good," Mrs. Webster said apologetically. "The Kanes are very private people. But Megan seemed like a nice, quiet girl."

"That family never took part in any of the neighborhood activities. Never played Bunko with us," Mr. Webster added. "Lots of isolated people like that nowadays."

"Did you ever talk to Mrs. Kane?" Cathy asked.

"Oh, my, no! She's a very shy person. I think she plays the piano. We always hear the piano when her husband and girl are away," Mrs. Webster said.

"Mrs. Kane is a pretty woman," Cathy said.

"Yes. She's from India, you know. It was such a shame when she fell and broke her nose. I wouldn't have known about it—but when the ambulance came to take her off, my maid heard from the Kane maid that she'd fallen and broken her nose. Her nose healed, but I notice there's a slight bump there now," Mrs. Webster said sympathetically.

When Cathy and Jeff were alone again in Jeff's car, Jeff said, "You know what, Cath? I think Mrs. Kane might be the key to all this. She acted like a robot on TV last night . . . but now I think I got it figured out. She's scared out of her wits. She's scared of him, her husband."

"Maybe he hit her and broke her nose," Cathy said.

"Yeah, that might explain why the kid took off. Imagine living in a house where the father terrorizes and beats the mother! The girl probably got so fed up with her mom taking it, not having the courage to bust out—" Jeff said.

"But Megan always seemed so well adjusted," Cathy objected.

"That's the way kids of abusive or alcoholic parents often are. They get so good at putting on an act that they almost fool *themselves*. These kids actually become different people when they're out in public," Jeff said.

"How do you know so much about this, Jeff?" Cathy asked in surprise. After all, he was trained as an engineer, not a social worker.

Jeff didn't answer right away, but then he said in a soft voice, "My sister was married to an abusive guy. But she put on such a good front for the family that we never guessed how bad it was. She'd come up with bruises and tell us fish stories about how clumsy she was. She'd actually make us *laugh* about it!

"*Doris the doofus.* That's what she called herself. And then one day her husband punched her real hard and she finally took off. But she was so embarrassed, she just vanished. By the time we found her, she'd made some bad friends and gotten on drugs. Worst of all, she never got out of that downward spiral. She died when she was only 27, an OD."

"Oh, Jeff, I'm sorry!" Cathy gasped.

"Happened a long time ago," he said.

They sat in Jeff's car until darkness fell. Then the maids started leaving. One of them came out of the Kane house around seven. As she was walking toward the bus stop, Cathy approached her. She asked the older woman if she was aware of any violence at the Kane house. Clearly, the woman didn't want to get involved. She shook her head and hurried away.

Finally, around nine, a weary looking woman with gray hair left the Kanes' house. Her feet were obviously hurting. She looked about 50 and was dark complected—perhaps also from India.

Cathy and Jeff got out of the car and followed her. "Ma'am," Cathy called to her. "We're private investigators, and we're trying to find Megan Marie. . . could you talk to us for a minute?"

"I don't understand what you want," the woman said in accented English.

"We just need to know if there's something *wrong* going on in that house. Something that could have driven the daughter to run away," Jeff said. He took some cash from his wallet. The woman looked poor—like she might badly need the extra money. "Could you help us?" he asked, holding out some bills toward the woman.

The maid's big, dark eyes settled on the cash. She had a sick, unemployed husband and two teenagers at home. It was hard to make ends meet on the minimum wages of a maid. She reached for the money and quietly put it into her purse. "Thank you," she said. "What I tell you is not from *me*, is that right?"

"Nobody will know it's from you," Cathy promised.

"That Mr. Kane," the woman said, "he is a devil."

Chapter 9

Cathy and Jeff looked at each other. Cathy's heart began racing. "Why do you say that?" she asked the maid.

"He screams at his poor wife until she can't stop shaking and sobbing. He tells her she is stupid. They got married when she was here in this country as a student. He was so rich. He promised her that she would be wealthy. She has many poor relatives back home. Her sisters needed help even to get married. *Dowries*, you know. Kane is like Ivan the Terrible—the wicked tyrant who ruled Russia," the maid said.

"Does he *hit* his wife?" Jeff asked.

"Often. Last spring he hit her and broke her nose. He wouldn't let her go to a doctor, so it healed funny. When I asked her why she puts up with it, she says it is for her family back home. They're often hungry, and they depend on the money she sends. Megan Marie was disgusted by her father. She put up a good act in front of everybody, but she hated what she saw happening to her mother," the maid said.

"How awful! Do you think Megan ran away because of what was going on?" Cathy asked.

"Kane never laid a hand on Megan. He didn't treat her badly—it was the mother who got the abuse. I often saw the girl sitting on the bed, pleading with her mother to call the hotline that helps abused women. But Mrs. Kane would cry and plead with Megan to keep her mouth shut. If the police came and took her husband away, she said that everything would be over. They would lose the house, he would lose his good job, and there would be no money for Megan's college, or for Mrs. Kane's family in India. Mrs. Kane got so hysterical that Megan never did call for help—and I think she hated herself for it," the maid said.

"But did Megan ever talk to her father about it?" Cathy asked.

"Oh, yes, many times. But then he gave her things, things she wanted very much. He gave her a trip to Europe with her grandmother when she was 14. He gave her a trip around the United States this past spring. And when she turned 16, he gave her that beautiful little red car. It cost tens of thousands of dollars, you know.

"Of course, Megan loved all those things very much. But still she ached for her mother. I think she was torn in two," the maid said. "Maybe she decided she couldn't stand to be torn in two anymore. Maybe that's why she ran away. I don't know. She was in a terrible predicament."

Jeff gave the maid another $20 bill,

and he and Cathy walked slowly over to where his car was parked.

"Well, do we have the answer?" he asked, looking concerned.

"I guess we know why she left, all right. But we still don't know where she is," Cathy said.

As they headed down the street, Cathy turned on the car radio. The top story was from New England. Senator Dean Mason had just gone up another ten points in the polls. When they got to Cathy's apartment, she and Jeff watched television for a little while. Senator Mason's face came on the screen. He was addressing a big crowd in a little town in New Hampshire. He *did* look something like President John Kennedy, Cathy thought. She had seen a lot of TV footage of Kennedy, and the same warmth and eye-twinkling smile could be seen on Mason's face.

"The guy has a good message," Jeff said. "Listen to him. He's demanding health care for the uninsured. And billions for research into deadly diseases."

Senator Mason's handsome face looked out from the television screen. "Isn't it at least as important to find a cure for cancer as it is to go to Mars?" he asked. "Isn't it more important to relieve the suffering of people dying from incurable diseases than it is to investigate black holes in space?"

"I like him," Cathy said.

The news anchor came on then. "Senator Mason will be in Portsmouth tomorrow to help dedicate a new shelter for abused spouses and children—a cause very dear to the senator's heart. As Mason often tells people, he spent his childhood in a foster home, a refugee from an abusive home himself."

Cathy turned to Jeff, her voice tense. "How far is it from here to Portsmouth, New Hampshire?" she asked.

Chapter 10

"About 200 miles," Jeff said. "If we leave right away we might be able to make it by the time the Senator gets there, Cath. Can you pack real fast?"

"Come back in 15 minutes," Cathy said. "I'll be ready."

They drove through the night, not talking much. But they arrived in plenty of time. Cathy and Jeff grabbed a ham and egg breakfast at a little cafe before they joined the people gathering at the new shelter for abused spouses.

It was just a wild hunch, but both Cathy and Jeff were going with it now. They waited in front of an old two-story house that had been refurbished. From now on it would serve as a temporary shelter for abused people on the run from dangerous situations. It was only a beginning, but it *was* a beginning. And Senator Mason was spearheading the whole thing.

A good crowd had gathered already. There were young volunteers wearing red, white, and blue t-shirts and caps. They passed out campaign literature and tried to warm up the crowd. Grandma had told Cathy that when President John Kennedy ran, the young volunteers were all out in force. Grandma said the enthusiasm of the kids was awesome. Cathy could feel that here, too.

Cathy and Jeff walked through the crowd, looking closely at every kid.

"Somehow I have a strong feeling that she came here," Cathy said. "She *must* be here. . . . "

Jeff shrugged. "I don't know, Cathy," he said uncertainly.

"There she is!" Cathy screamed. "Over there! Look, Jeff! She's the girl with the sunglasses on."

Cathy rushed over to the girl, with Jeff bringing up the rear. "Oh, Megan! Thank God you're okay! I've been so worried about you."

Megan Marie's jaw dropped in shock. Then big tears spilled down her cheeks. "I'm so s-sorry, Ms. North. I guess I should've told you—but I knew you'd try to stop me! I guess anybody would have. But I had to cut out of there. I just *had* to!" Megan cried.

"I understand. I know what's been going on with your parents. I know what you're running from," Cathy said.

Megan's eyes widened. "I've been living on money I saved from Christmas gifts. We get freebies to eat at the campaign stops, and I've just slept wherever I can put down a sleeping bag," she said.

"Oh, Megan, the police are dragging the lake and everybody's looking for you," Cathy said.

"I ditched the car because it meant so

much to me. For a long time, my father kept me home by giving me stuff. I finally realized that I had sold my soul for that car—along with the trips and the great clothes!

"But finally, I had enough. I just couldn't stand around and watch Mom lose her self-respect anymore. That's why I made my voice sound funny when I called you. I wanted you to tell my father that I was really gone. I thought it would shake him up, maybe make him change, or something," Megan said. "But I guess Dad hasn't changed, huh?"

Cathy shook her head. "He's blaming *me* for putting rebellious ideas in your head, " she said sadly.

Megan wiped her tears away with the back of her hand. "I'll go back and let everybody know what happened. It's time to face the music. But I'm not going back to that house—not ever! I'll go live with my grandma," she said.

Cathy put her arm around Megan

Marie and led her gently back toward the car. In the distance, Senator Mason's motorcade was arriving. Everybody was cheering. Megan Marie turned around to look at him, and a brave, hopeful smile lit up her face.

COMPREHENSION QUESTIONS

RECALL

1. Why was Cathy North so concerned about Megan Marie's absence from school?

2. What did Mr. Kane do to ensure his daughter's silence about what was happening at home?

3. Where did Cathy and Jeff finally find Megan?

VOCABULARY

1. Mr. Kane accused Cathy North of "pushing her radical political agenda." What's a *radical political agenda*? Explain the term and give an example.

2. The TV interviewer said that Mr. and Mrs. Kane were "distraught." What does *distraught* mean? Name some synonyms.

3. Mr. Kane made serious "allegations" against Cathy North. What are *allegations*? Explain and name some synonyms.

ANALYZING CHARACTERS

1. Which two words could be used to describe Cathy North? Explain your thinking.
   - *geriatric*
   - *determined*
   - *enthusiastic*

2. Which two words could be used to describe Mr. Kane? Give examples.
   - *gruff*
   - *honorable*
   - *intimidating*

3. Which two words could be used to describe Megan Marie? Explain your thinking.
   - *frustrated*
   - *idealistic*
   - *wayward*

DRAWING CONCLUSIONS

1. Why did Wendy Birdsong give Cathy North such unfair treatment in her TV interview?

2. Why did Mrs. Kane put up with her husband's abuse?